The
DENSLOW
PICTURE BOOK
TREASURY

The DENSLOW PICTURE BOOK TREASURY

W. W. DENSLOW

With an Introduction by
MICHAEL PATRICK HEARN

DOVER PUBLICATIONS, INC.
MINEOLA, NEW YORK

Bibliographical Note

The Denslow Picture Book Treasury, first published by Dover Publications, Inc., in 2010, is a new selection of stories and illustrations from the following sources: *Denslow's Humpty Dumpty,* published by G. W. Dillingham Co., New York, 1903 *(Humpty Dumpty); Denslow's Humpty Dumpty and Other Stories,* published by G. W. Dillingham Co., New York, 1903 *(Little Red Riding-Hood, The Three Bears, Mary Had a Little Lamb, Old Mother Hubbard,* and *The House That Jack Built);* and *Denslow's One Ring Circus and Other Stories,* published by M. A. Donohue and Company, Chicago, 1903 *(The One Ring Circus, The Zoo,* and *5 Little Pigs).* An Introduction by Michael Patrick Hearn has been written specially for the Dover edition.

Library of Congress Cataloging-in-Publication Data

Denslow, W. W. (William Wallace), 1856–1915.
    The Denslow picture book treasury / W. W. Denslow ; with an introduction by Michael Patrick Hearn. — Dover ed.
        p. cm.
    Summary: A collection of nine tales originally published in 1903 in three collections, Denslow's Humpty Dumpty, Denslow's Humpty Dumpty and Other Stories, and Denslow's One Ring Circus and Other Stories.
    Contents: Humpty Dumpty — Little Red Riding Hood — The three bears — Mary had a little lamb — Old Mother Hubbard — The house that Jack built — The one ring circus — The zoo — 5 little pigs.
    ISBN-13: 978-0-486-47917-0
    ISBN-10: 0-486-47917-X
    1. Children's stories, American. 2. Nursery rhymes. 3. Fairy tales. [1. Short stories. 2. Nursery rhymes. 3. Fairy tales.] I. Title. II. Title: Picture book treasury.
PZ7.D434Ddp 2010
[E]—dc22

2010024281

Manufactured in the United States by Courier Corporation
47917X01
www.doverpublications.com

Contents

INTRODUCTION

Michael Patrick Hearn

In 1903 and 1904, with the publication of *Denslow's Picture Books for Children*, William Wallace Denslow (1856–1915) reached the crest of the wave of his popularity as America's leading children's book illustrator. He produced a runaway bestseller, in his first collaboration with L. Frank Baum, *Father Goose, His Book* (1899), and he insured his place in American literary history with their second effort, *The Wonderful Wizard of Oz* (1900). The response to their last work, *Dot and Tot of Merryland* (1901), was not stellar, but the artist returned to the forefront of the juvenile book trade with the bestselling *Denslow's Mother Goose* (1901) and *Denslow's Night Before Christmas* (1902). These were not just *any* editions: they were *Denslow's*. He had become so widely known as America's preeminent children's book illustrator that his dependable name alone in the title assured success.

In September 1902, W. W. Denslow signed a lucrative contract with the G. W. Dillingham Company of New York to produce the series *Denslow's Picture Books for Children*. These were to be up-to-date equivalents of the popular cheaply produced toy books issued by George Routledge and Sons in London and McLoughlin Brothers in New York during the late nineteenth century. These works generally were retellings of popular nursery rhymes and tales, frequently illustrated with gaudy full-color pictures. During this same period emerged the elegant work of the great English picture-book artists Walter Crane, Kate Greenaway, Randolph Caldecott, and L. Leslie Brooke. These artists approached the form as individual works of art in which every element of the book's design—covers, endpapers, title, dedication, copyright, and the rest—contributed to the subtle aesthetic harmony of the whole. Denslow built on these high artistic standards in his own publications for children.

Denslow produced most of the work in the "Picture Books" in Bermuda. Having suffered a physical breakdown in 1901 due to overwork and been confined briefly that year to a sanitarium, the illustrator was advised to spend the winter of 1902 to 1903 in the "Land of the Lilies." "Here everything is peaceful and I am well content," he reported to famed photographer Alfred Stieglitz. "I can work calmly and rationally with fair health (on the improve all the time)." Any time he needed to escape the rigors of modern life, he could just "slip away . . . on a swift sailing craft, to the coral reefs that surround the islands and there see the mighty, generous and graceful Hand of God above and below the sea." The climate invigorated Denslow, and he was never more productive than during his stay at the Hotel Inverurie in Hamilton, Bermuda.

He completed the series back in his studio in New York City. "It was as good as a three-ring circus to see Den at work designing and making his drawings," reported an old friend, the newspaperman Charles Waldron. "He would have a different [pencil] sketch tacked on to different boards. . . . When one drawing became tiresome he would work on another. In order to get the right action . . . the figure might have as many as six different legs, four heads, and as many arms. When the right ones were selected . . . they would be drawn in with ink and the others erased." Denslow always drew his pictures in black India ink, adding the colors later in consultation with the printers. He was sure to sign every illustration with his well-known monogram, "Den," and his stylized seahorse.

The public got its first glimpse of this latest project on December 14, 1902, in the prestigious New York *Sunday Herald*. For its special holiday supplement, the artist not only illustrated but also retold a quartet of *Denslow's Christmas Tales* in harmless doggerel: "Red Riding Hood," "Humpty Dumpty, Jr," "The Three Bears," and "Jack and the Beanstalk." The following year, he reworked these stories in prose as individual volumes in the first series of *Denslow's Picture Books for Children*.

In October 1903, Dillingham published an even dozen of toy books: *Denslow's Humpty Dumpty, Little Red Riding Hood, The Three Bears, Mary Had a Little Lamb, Old Mother Hubbard, House That Jack Built, The One Ring Circus, The Zoo, 5 Little Pigs, Tom Thumb, A B C Book,* and *Jack and the Bean-Stalk*. This first series sold so well that six more were issued in 1904: *Denslow's Three Little Kittens, Mother Goose ABC Book, Barnyard Circus, Animal Fair, Simple Simon,* and *Scarecrow and the Tin Man*. Each oversized pamphlet comprised twelve full-color pages, printed on fine egg-shell-colored paper and bound in sturdy wrappers. Dillingham issued the entire series in three formats: the regular trade edition of the individual eighteen pamphlets at 25 cents each; an "indestructible" version mounted on linen at 50 cents each; and three clothbound collections of six titles each for $1.25: *Denslow's One Ring Circus and Other Stories* and *Denslow's Humpty Dumpty and Other Stories*, both in 1903, and *Denslow's Scarecrow and the Tin-Man and Other Stories* in 1904.

While the works of Crane, Caldecott, and Brooke resembled the British toy books in format and content, Denslow was perhaps more conscious of his young audience than were those famous English illustrators. Whereas Crane wanted to elevate the taste of children, Denslow catered to their young capabilities. Some of Caldecott's texts (such as William Cowper's "The Diverting History of John Gilpin," "Elegy on the Death of a Mad Dog," and "Mrs. Mary Blaize") were not written for children in the first place. Denslow's picture books were free of the dainty prettiness so characteristic of Greenaway's enormously popular illustrations. He was perhaps most in harmony with Brooke's methods, but his attitude towards the picture book was thoroughly modern—and thoroughly American.

Denslow, unlike his talented predecessors, appealed directly to the girls and boys themselves. He knew exactly how to entertain them. "From the kids you can always get unbiased criticism," he reported. "They don't play favorites, and there is no way you can tamper with the witnesses. They like a thing, or they don't. And if they like it, they demand more of it." That had certainly been the case with *Father Goose, The Wizard of Oz, Mother Goose,* and *Night Before Christmas.* "I'd rather please the kids than any audience in the world," he confessed. "If I can reach them . . . I ask for little more." He also slyly acknowledged, "It has been my experience that when you reach the youngsters you can reach their elders also."

Denslow's robust interpretation of the classics provided a refreshing antidote to the common anemic picture books of the period. "My aim in children's pictures and verse is to furnish good, clean wholesome fun for children, eliminating the deceit, murder and theft that is so rife in the older fairy tales," he explained. "These elements bore harmful results. A child reading of downright treachery and cruelty does not recognize the wrong of it, but deems it proper and worthy of imitation. Anyhow, keep this spirit out of the stories, verse and pictures that children read and you never contribute injurious ideas." The artist was the first to admit, "When I illustrate and edit childhood classics I do not hesitate to expurgate."

He was hardly the first to revise the old nursery rhymes and tales according to vicissitudes of popular taste; he likely had in mind L. Frank Baum's principles as defined in the introduction to *The Wizard of Oz.* Baum called for the establishment of a new juvenile literature "in which the wonderment and joy are retained and the heartaches and nightmares are left out." This literature must differ from that of earlier children's books by being free of all "horrible and blood-curdling incident devised by their authors to point a fearsome moral to each tale." He insisted, "The modern child seeks only entertainment in its wonder tales and gladly dispenses with all disagreeable incident." Denslow too was determined to supply new nursery lore for the twentieth century. "The fairy tales of the modern day are gradually following the new standards and the effect on the youngsters who read this better class of juvenile writing, is even now appreciable," he admitted. "They are growing up into wholesome, sane maturity, free from the bugaboos, the horrors and fear inspired by the older type of writing that exulted in piled up impressions of barbarity." To defend his methods, he said, "I don't think I make anything namby-pamby, nor do I eliminate the funny element in the work. I do not hesitate to say that where I illustrate and edit the childhood classics they will be expurgated editions and the children will not suffer from it one bit." Neither Grandmother nor Little Red Riding Hood is eaten up in the Denslow version of the old French fairy tale. Just as the wolf is about to pounce upon the child, the old woman shows up and beats him into submission with her walking stick; having taught him a painful lesson, she turns the now docile animal into the family watchdog. Denslow's Golden Hair is no longer the little snoop of the popular nursery story. Instead of causing all kinds of havoc in the home of the Three Bears, the little girl tidies up the place before they return; and all four become great pals after that.

While the traditional rhymes "The House That Jack Built" and "5 Little Pigs" were reprinted largely unadulterated, Denslow looked up the original little-known full texts of Sarah Josepha Hale's "Mary's Lamb" and Sarah Catherine Martin's "The Comic Adventures of Old Mother Hubbard and Her Dog." The latter, however, required some revision, so Denslow removed all references to death and coffins, and smoking and drinking. He then added two more child-friendly verses:

She went to the butcher's | She went to the market
To buy him a chop, | To buy him some fish,
And when she came back | And when she got back
He was spinning a top. | He was licking the dish.

Denslow composed a new story around the familiar riddle of Humpty Dumpty just as Baum had done in *Mother Goose in Prose* (1897). The artist introduced the *son* of the famous nursery character and made sure the egg was hard-boiled before he set off on his adventures. (The son slightly resembles the famous white-faced clown George L. Fox billed as "The Original Humpty Dumpty" in his legendary musical pantomime of 1868.) Denslow's *Zoo* and *One Ring Circus* presented wholly original stories invented by the illustrator himself about little Peter Funnybones in the Glad Lands. Denslow then dedicated each volume to the child of a dear friend; for example, *Little Red Riding Hood* honored Cornelia Otis Skinner, the young daughter of actor Otis Skinner.

Whatever vigor might have been lost in revising the texts was more than made up for in the sunny, cheery pictures. Denslow was first and foremost a *comic* illustrator. "To make children laugh," he explained, "you must tell them stories of action. They aren't really fascinated by cruelty—it's action they want. The trouble is that their desires have been misunderstood." His little figures are always acting and reacting, their eager faces bright with wonder and delight. Every single inhabitant of the Glad Lands seems to be greatly enjoying him or herself. "Action, children demand," Denslow said, "and you can give them plenty of wholesome action, fun and entertainment without ever employing the easier trick of crowding force into your humor by impressions of brutality, cunning, deceit or the shock of horror and gore."

Denslow's menagerie was entirely benign. His lions and tigers and bears were never so dangerous, never so fierce as those in their original sources. Denslow's comic animals were the result of a subtle study of comparative anatomy. He could express the entire range of human emotion in his charming beasts, birds, and fish. "I tell my stories with pictures," he argued, "and I can often indicate action by expression. Action and expression, then, are two of my mainstays, and when you add the incongruous, you have the triad on which I rely."

He always infused his lively pictures with "pure wit and clean fun." The humor was often broad and perfectly suited to the taste of youngsters. For example, he cleverly undercut the tension of Little Red Riding Hood's first encounter with the old gray wolf by having the trees in the forest smile fondly on her. "No real harm will come to pass," they seem to be saying. Denslow also included some private jokes in his pictures, such as depicting L. Frank Baum as the policeman in *5 Little Pigs*. Another familiar face can be spotted in the farmer's cornfield in *House That Jack Built*—the beloved Scarecrow from *The Wizard of Oz*.

The reviews of Denslow's works were almost uniformly positive. "No better presents have been designed this season for small folk than 'Denslow's Picture Books for Children,'" declared *The Dial*, "twelve paper-covered booklets in the newest and best manner of Mr. William Wallace Denslow." *Publishers Weekly* pronounced them "among the most original quartos of that season." As *The Critic* announced in January 1904, "There is no more popular caterer to young people's tastes than Mr. Denslow." *The Literary World* predicted that these picture books "will bring joy to many a youngster."

The most elaborate critique of the series was provided by the critic and editor Joseph Moore Bowles in the influential Chicago art journal *Brush and Pencil* in September 1903. He called W. W. Denslow "an impressionist for babies" who "omits all but fundamentals and essentials." Having worked as an important poster designer of the 1890s, Denslow knew how to reduce his compositions to their basic geometry. No gratuitous details distract the young eye from the central action of each picture. His bold bounding black line plays gracefully against squares, circles, and rectangles of bright flat color. "Den's panels, circles and spots, and his solid pages of gorgeous hues with perhaps one tiny figure or object in a lower corner are simply baits to catch [the child's] attention," said Bowles. He reported seeing "a baby of months beam with delight as some of the pages were turned, and fairly jump at color deliberately placed by the crafty Mr. Denslow, who knows how to arouse those little emotions."

In 1913, the Chicago publisher M. A. Donohue and Co. secured the plates of *Denslow's Picture Books for Children* and reissued them in various forms into the 1920s. Thereafter, the series all but disappeared for sixty years and was generally forgotten except among connoisseurs of rare children's books. Now Dover Publications has issued a delightful collection of the first nine titles as a sturdy paperback, *The Denslow Picture Book Treasury*. Denslow's "Picture Books" are as bright, fresh, and entertaining as ever and will no doubt continue to delight the little ones—and their elders—for many years to come.

The
DENSLOW
PICTURE BOOK
TREASURY

Humpty Dumpty.

HUMPTY-DUMPTY was a smooth, round little chap, with a winning smile, and a great golden heart in his broad breast.

Only one thing troubled Humpty, and that was, that he might fall and crack his thin, white skin; he wished to be hard, all the way through, for he felt his heart wabble when he walked, or ran about, so off he went to the Black Hen for advice.

This Hen was kind and wise, so she was just the one, for him to go to with his trouble.

"Your father, Old Humpty," said the

Hen, "was very foolish, and would take warning from no one; you know what the poet said of him:

'Humpty=Dumpty sat on a wall,
Humpty=Dumpty had a great fall;
All the king's horses, and all the king's men
Cannot put Humpty=Dumpty together again.'

"So you see, he came to a very bad end, just because he was reckless, and would not take a hint from any one, he was much worse than a scrambled egg; the king, his horses and his men, did all they could for him, but his case was

2

hopeless," and the Hen shook her head
sadly.

"What you must do," continued the
Hen, as she wiped a tear from her bright
blue eye, "is to go to the Farmer's Wife,
next door, and tell her to put you into
a pot of boiling hot water; your skin
is so hard and smooth, it will not hurt
you, and when you come out, you may

do as you wish, nothing can break you, you can tumble about to your heart's content, and you will not break, nor even dent yourself."

So Humpty rolled in next door, and told the Farmer's Wife that he wanted to be put into boiling hot water as he was too brittle to be of any use to himself or to any one else.

"Indeed you shall," said the Farmer's Wife, "what is more I shall wrap you up in a piece of spotted calico, so that you will have a nice colored dress; you will come out, looking as bright as an Easter Egg."

So she tied him up in a gay new rag, and dropped him into the copper kettle of boiling water that was on the hearth.

It was pretty hot for Humpty at first, but he soon got used to it, and was happy, for he felt himself getting harder every minute.

He did not have to stay in the water long, before he was quite well done, and as hard as a brick all the way through; so, untying the rag, he jumped out of the kettle as tough and as bright as any hard boiled Egg.

The cal=ico had marked him from head to foot with big, bright, red spots, he was as

gaudy as a circus clown, and as nimble and merry as one.

The Farmer's Wife shook with laughter to see the pranks of the little fellow, for he frolicked and frisked about from table to chair, and mantelpiece; he would fall from the shelf to the floor, just to show how hard he was; and after thanking the good woman most politely, for the service she had done him, he walked out into the sunshine, on the clothes=line, like a rope dancer, to see the wide, wide world.

*　　　　*　　　　*　　　　*

Of the travels of Humpty-Dumpty much could be said; he went East, West, North and South; he sailed the seas, he walked and rode on the land through all the Countries of the Earth, and all his life long he was happy and content.

Sometimes as a clown, in a circus, he would make fun for old and young; again, as a wandering minstrel, he

twanged the strings of his banjo and sung a merry song, and so on through all his travels, he would lighten the cares of others, and make them forget their sorrows,

and fill every heart with joy.

But wherever he went, in sunshine or in rain, he never forgot to sing the praises of the wise Black Hen nor the good, kind Farmer's Wife, who had started him in life, *hardened* against sorrow, with a big heart in the **right** place, for the cheer and comfort of OTHERS.

Little Red Riding-Hood

The forest was bright with the many colored leaves of autumn, as Little Red Riding Hood tripped merrily along the woodland path, toward her grandmother's cottage, two or more miles from her own house, with a basket of good things for the old lady.

There were cheese cakes, honey, some oolong tea, ginger=bread, and many little dainty tid=bits that the good grandmother could not get in her far away home.

Little Red Riding Hood was a favorite child of the fairies, so no harm could ever come to her, and she was a friend of all the little song birds in the wild wood, so that they came and twittered to her, and she talked to them, in their own language, as she went gaily on her way.

"Good morning, Red Riding Hood," said the gaunt gray wolf, as he stood in her path, and sniffed at her basket, "what have you there?"

"Some cheese cakes and sweets, for granny dear," said she, "so get out of my way, and let me go on, for I must hurry." She did not like the hungry look of the wolf, nor the gleam of his cruel looking teeth, when he smiled and tried to look pleasant.

It made the hungry wolf's mouth water, when he heard of all those good things, and as he was a greedy robber, he had a great mind to take them away from Riding Hood, and eat them up. But when he heard the ring of the woodman's ax, as  he chopped at the sturdy oaks, near by, he was afraid that a call from Riding Hood would get him into trouble, so, as he was a crafty old wolf, he simply said, with a smile,

"Why certainly, my dear, run right along to granny. I hope you will find her well."

But no sooner was she out of sight than off he flew, by a short cut, to the cottage of the grandmother, for he was bound to have that good dinner if he could get it.

Loudly he knocked on the door and as there was no answer, he pulled the latch string, and went sneaking in.

"Granny isn't here," he said to himself, "now I will have it all my own way, and get that basket of good things

too. I'll just put on this night=cap and gown, that are hanging here, and when Riding Hood comes in and puts the basket down, I will jump up and growl and snap my teeth; she will be frightened, of course, and run away, then I will have the cakes and sweets to myself."

No sooner said than done, and when he had climbed in between the clean white sheets of the bed, and pulled the night=cap well over his long nose, you could not have told the wicked old gray wolf from a nice old lady.

Just as he expected, in came Little Red Riding Hood with a bound, she marched right up to the bed, and said:

"Why, grandma, dear, why are you in bed this beauti= ful day?"

"I'm not feeling very well, my dear," said the wolf, in as mild a voice as a wolf could use.

"My! my! what a hoarse voice you have," said the girl.

"I have a cold, my dear," said the wolf, and his greedy eyes shone bright under the night=cap.

"Goodness! how fierce your eyes look, and what big sharp teeth you have, dear grandmamma," said Riding Hood.

"The better to see, and to eat up your good sweets with, and you too, if you don't keep still," growled the wolf, as he sprang out of bed; but as he jumped he got all tangled up in the night gown, and went fliperty=flop on the floor, where, the more he kicked to get free from the clothes, the more he got wrapped up in them.

"No, you don't," said the stout old grandmother, who had

come softly in as he made his last speech, "I'll teach you to put on my night clothes, and get into my nice bed," she hit him a sounding whack on the head  with her walking stick; crack! and she belabored him over the back; she got the sneaking old gray wolf up in a corner, and beat him until he howled for mercy.

Then she chained him to a post outside in the garden, where the little girl went up to him, and said, "Now will you be good?" and left him to think it over.

It was a jolly little lunch, that the child and the old lady sat down to, that day, with the cheese cakes and sweetmeats from the basket, that had been so nearly lost, and they lingered long over the tea cups, chatting and trying to think of some way to reform the wolf and make him useful.

When lunch was finally over Little Red Riding Hood went out and had a long talk with the wolf.

He seemed subdued by the beating, and he promised faithfully to be good and to always do as he was bid, if they would feed him, and not tell the woodmen about what he had done, for he was afraid they would hunt him down, and kill him, if they knew he had been so wicked.

So the little girl sent word, by the woodmen, that she would not be home for a few days, but would stay with her grand=mother to keep her company.

She then devoted herself to teaching the wolf to be good, useful and amusing.

The first thing she taught him, was to sit up and beg for his meals, and never to steal anything to eat.

Beside she showed him many tricks to amuse; he would sit up, stand on his hind legs and walk, he would lie down and roll over, in fact he would do anything that Riding Hood told him.

At night he guarded the house so well, that

no robbers or tramps would dare come near the place.

When she was ready to go home, she hitched the wolf to a funny little cart, the woodmen had made for her, and bid= ding her grandmamma, good=bye, she started, like a little princess, in her carriage.

Great was the surprise of the master woodman and his wife to see their little daughter come home in a cart drawn by the gaunt gray wolf, they greeted her with joy and treated the wolf well.

Little Red Riding Hood named the wolf, Towser, and sent him to his friends in the wild wood to tell them how well he was treated, and what a good time he had at the home of Riding Hood, so many wolves came, and lived in the cottages of the woodmen and farmers of that country and proved to be useful.

And it is to this little girl, of the olden time, so long ago, we owe our thanks, for giving to us, that trusty and faithful friend;—THE DOG.

THE THREE BEARS.

A LONG time ago in a cottage on the edge of a great forest there dwelt a little girl by the name of Golden Hair; she was an orphan and lived with her grandmother who loved her dearly. The grandmother was very old and so most of the house work was done by Golden Hair; but she was so young and strong she did not mind that a bit, for she had plenty of time to play and was merry the whole day long.

Although little Golden Hair lived far from other children she was never lone= some, for she had many friends and play=

mates in the wild creatures of the wood. The gentle, soft eyed deer would feed from her hand, and the wild birds would come at her musical call; for she knew their language and loved them well.

Golden Hair had never wandered far into the forest. But one day in the early autumn time, as she was gathering bright leaves and golden rod, she strayed farther than she knew and came upon a lonely, gray cabin under the mighty trees. A slab of wood be= side the half open door told who lived within. It read:

"Papa Bear, Mamma Bear, and the Tiny Bear."

"So this is where the jolly bears live!" said Golden Hair, as she knocked upon the door. "I want to meet them."

No answer came to her knocking, so she pushed the door wide open and walked in.

It was a most disorderly house, but a bright fire burned on the hearth, over which hung a big, black kettle of bubbling soup, while on the table, near by, were three yellow bowls of different sizes.

"A big bowl for Papa Bear, a medium sized bowl for Mamma Bear, and a little bowl for the Tiny Bear," said Golden Hair.

"That soup smells good," she went on to say, "but my! what an untidy house! I'll put the place to rights while I am waiting for the bears to come home."

So she
went to
work to sweep and
dust and soon had the
room in order. Then she
went into the bed room and
made up the three beds: the big
one for Papa Bear,
the medium sized
one for Mamma
Bear, and
the little
one for the
Tiny Bear;
she bustled
and had every=
thing as neat as
a pin when in bounced the three
jolly bears. For a moment the
bears stood speechless, with wide

open eyes, staring at Golden Hair, who stood, like a ray of sunshine in the dusky room; then they burst into loud laughter and made her welcome to their home. When they saw how nice and clean it was they thanked her heartily and invited her to share their dinner, for the soup was now ready and they were all hungry. Golden Hair spent the rest of the day with the three jolly bears playing "hi spy" and many new games which the bears taught her.

When the afternoon sun was sinking in the west the little girl said she must be getting home, for her grandma would be anxious about her. The three bears would not let her go alone, so they all set off together through the twilight woods,—a merry company.

Golden Hair rode upon the broad back of Papa Bear, while Mamma Bear and Tiny walked gaily on either side. In this way, before night had fallen, they came clear of the wood and up to the home of Golden Hair.

To be sure the grandmother was much surprised to see

this shaggy company with her little Golden
Hair; but when she saw how jolly they
all were and how handy they were in
helping Golden Hair get the supper, she was
delighted to have them stay, and gave
them welcome. Papa Bear split the wood,
brought it in, and built the fire; Mamma
Bear got the tea kettle and filled it with
water that was carried from the well by the
Tiny Bear, and soon they were able to sit down
to a good supper of hot
biscuit, wild honey and

pumpkin pie, with tea for the elders and nice sweet milk for Golden Hair and the Tiny Bear.

The grandmother liked the three bears so well and the bears were so delighted with the comforts of home that they all decided to live together for the general good.

Papa Bear would do the chores and stand guard over the house at night; Mamma Bear  would do the housework under the direc= tion of Golden Hair, while the Tiny Bear would wait upon grandmother and run errands for the household.

And so it came about that the three bears moved their three bowls and their

three beds to the home of Golden Hair and her grandmother, the very next day; and from all accounts they were happy ever after. At any rate the fame of Golden Hair and the three bears spread far and wide through all the countryside, so that on holidays troops of children came to play with the four jolly friends.

The good natured bears were always anxious to please the children; they would get up games under the green= wood trees in the summer, and merry sports upon the icy lake or snowy hills in winter. They did their best to make life for all, one glad round of joy. Just how long they lived thus, no one seems to know; for it was a long, long time ago and nothing is left but a joyous memory of a happy golden time.

Mary had a little lamb;

     Its fleece was white as snow;

And everywhere that Mary went,

     The lamb was sure to go.

It followed her to school one day,

Which was against the rule;

It made the children laugh and play

To see the lamb at school.

And so the teacher turned it out;

But still it lingered near,

And waited patiently about

Till Mary did appear.

And then it ran to her, and laid

        Its head upon her arm;

As if to say, "I'm not afraid.

        You'll keep me from all harm."

"What makes the lamb love Mary so?"

The eager children cry;

"Oh, Mary loves the lamb, you know,"

The teacher did reply.

And you each gentle animal

To you for life may bind,

And make them follow at your call

If you are only kind.

Old Mother Hubbard.

Old mother Hubbard
Went to the cupboard
　　　To get her poor dog a bone;
But when she came there,
The cupboard was bare,
　　　And so the poor dog had none.

She went to the
butcher's
To get him a chop,
And when she came back
He was spinning a top.

She went
    to the market
        To buy him some fish,
And when she came back
        He was licking the dish.

She went up to town

        To buy him a bed,

And when she came back

        He stood on his head.

She went to the hatter's

To buy him a hat,

But when she came back

He was feeding the cat.

She went to the barber's

        To buy him **a** wig,

But when she came back

        He was dancing a jig.

She went to the fruiterer's

    To buy him some fruit,

But when she came back

    He was playing the flute.

She went to the tailor's

To buy him a coat,

But when she came back

He was riding a goat.

She went to the cobbler's

    To buy him some shoes,

But when she came back

    He was reading the news.

She went to the
    hosier's
       To buy him some hose,
But when she came back
       He was dressed in his clothes.

The dame made a curtsey,

The dog made a bow;

The dame said, "Your servant;"

The dog said, "Bow, wow."

This is the house
that Jack built.

This is the malt

That lay in the house that Jack built.

This is the rat
That ate the malt
That lay in the
house that
Jack built.

This is the cat,

That caught the rat,

That ate the malt

That lay in the house

        that Jack built.

This is the dog,

That worried the cat,

That caught the rat,

That ate the malt

That lay in the house

        that Jack built.

This is the cow with

the crumpled horn,

That tossed the dog,

That worried the cat,

That caught the rat,

That ate the malt

That lay in the house

that Jack built.

This is the maiden all forlorn,
That milked the cow
        with the crumpled horn,
That tossed the dog,
    That worried the cat,
      That caught the rat,
      That ate the malt
      That lay in the house
        that Jack built.

This is the man all tattered and torn,
That kissed the maiden all forlorn,
That milked the cow
  with the crumpled horn,
That tossed the dog,
That worried the cat,
That caught
          the rat,
That ate the malt
That lay
  in the house
    that Jack built.

This is the priest all shaven and shorn,

That married the man all tattered and torn,

That kissed the maiden all forlorn,

That milked the cow with the crumpled horn,

That tossed the dog,

That worried the cat,

That caught the rat,

That ate the malt

That lay in the house

that

Jack built.

This is the cock that crowed
in the morn,
That waked the priest
all shaven and shorn,
That married the man
all tattered and torn,
That kissed the maiden all forlorn,
That milked the cow
with the
crumpled horn,
That tossed the dog,
That worried the cat,
That caught the rat,
That ate the malt
That lay in the
house that
Jack built.

This is the farmer sowing his corn,

That kept the cock

that crowed in the morn,

That waked the priest

all shaven and shorn,

That married the man

all tattered and torn,

That kissed the maiden all forlorn,

That milked the cow with

the crumpled horn,

That tossed the dog,

That worried the cat,

That caught the rat,

That ate the malt

That lay in the

house that

Jack built.

The One Ring Circus.

ONE balmy day in June, Peter Funny=bone was up on top of the straw=stack listening to the thrush's song and the hum of bees, which came to him from the clover patch, back of the barn.

As he lay on his back watching the lazy cotton clouds drift across the sky of blue, he suddenly heard a great com=motion in the barn=yard below him; the shouting of men, the tramp of horses, all mingled with the music of a band.

On looking over the edge of the high stack a most wonderful sight was before him of strange animals and many people in gay fantastic dress.

Jokes were passed and laughter rang out upon the summer air, while they all bustled about, preparing for some great event.

"What are you all doing here?" asked Peter of a clown in gay, baggy clothes, who stood below him.

"This," said the clown, "is Hunkey Dorey's Circus, the greatest show on earth. I am the human programme," and, with a double sumersault, he was beside the boy upon the stack.

"Hankey! Pankey! presto, change!" cried the clown, clapping his hands, and, in a jiffy, Peter Funnybone and the clown were whirled high in the air and landed on the broad back of the great gray elephant that stood near. He had picked them up in his long trunk and put them there.

The elephant was guided by a little brown boy in white, with a red sash, and he drove right for the big barn doors, which flew open as they came near, show= ing beyond, a great circus tent packed with people, who gave a mighty shout as the elephant rolled into the ring.

The clown stood up and shouted in a voice of brass:—

"The elephant now goes 'round,
The band begins to play,
And the boys around the monkey's cage
Had better get out of the way."

The elephant tossed Peter and the clown onto a high platform, at the other side of the ring, and took his place at the head of the grand march, that was entering.

The Queen of Beauty headed the procession in her golden chariot, drawn by two white camels of the desert. She was followed by a long train of gaily dressed ladies and brave knights in

armor of gold and silver, bearing banners of silk on long lances. Following, came Bedouins on pure white Arabian steeds, covered with gay trappings of silk and gems. Nubians followed on coal=black horses; and after, came people of all foreign lands, mounted on horses of every color—a gay and glittering throng.

The bright lights, flashing on the pol=ished metals and cloths of every shade and color, made a picture too dazzling to describe.

A trumpet blew and like magic the ring was cleared. In rushed a crowd of funny clowns, with trained donkeys, pigs, cats, and goats.

The antics of the clowns, and the tricks of the animals, made Peter Funnybone and the whole, great crowd shout for joy.

Next came the bare-back riders, all champions of the world; beautiful girls in gauzy skirts, and brave swarthy men on wild, fiery, untamed steeds of Tartary, which they urged to their utmost speed, while they made airy flights through burning hoops or over silken banners held by clowns and grooms.

The tall ring=master was there, and funny men by scores, tight=rope dancers, jugglers from far Japan, leapers and vaulters who somersaulted over scores of horses and elephants, a troupe of trained zebras with monkeys for riders, and cow=boys and Indians from the wild and woolly west. Then came the band=master with whiskers, and the medals on his chest, who was cheered and cheered again, as the ring=master pinned another badge upon his back.

Peter Funnybone was in his glory, for all of these things were explained to him by

the human pro= gramme who sat beside him. There was only one thing he did not like. A most impolite little jaybird perched upon the back of his chair, and every now and then, would switch its tail about and tickle him in the ear, just as he was enjoying something very much. He would drive the bird away, but it always returned.

The music ceased; a bell sounded from far away; fairy boys and girls all dressed in yellow, red and green, mounted upon giant butterflies, were trooping into the ring, and Peter leaned forward to get a better view.

*   *   *   *   *   *

Just then, he sat up on the straw=stack, wide awake, as the cheery voice of his sister Sue struck his ear.

"Wake up, you lazy boy! I have been tickling your ear with a straw for the last five minutes, trying to wake you. Don't you hear the supper bell?"

The Zoo.

O N an Indian Summer morn=ing Peter Funnybone and his sister Sue were sitting among the golden rod and long grass, in the back part of the orchard.

Peter was drawing pictures of ani=mals, and telling Sue stories about all the strange and wonderful things he had seen at the Zoo.

"That's a pretty good picture of a hippopotamus," said a voice from behind them, "but I can show you the real thing."

The voice came from an ostrich, who had seated himself close to the pair and was beaming down on them with his kindly, comical face.

"Yes," said the bird, "you get on my back, and I will take you to the Glad Lands, on the slope of Merry Mountain, where the birds and animals have a Zoo of their own, and are happy all day long, year in and year out."

It was easy for Sue and Peter to climb on the back of the ostrich, as he was seated, but when the mam= moth bird rose to his full height, they were far above the ground.

"Hold on tight, for this is an express train," said the ostrich, and off he went at a run, as fast as his long legs could carry him.

Over hill and dale they went at lightning speed, jumping rivers and hopping streams. But the motion was so even and pleasant that the children enjoyed every minute of the ride, as they rose over mountains or skimmed lightly across vast level and sandy deserts and tract=less wastes.

For miles and miles they traveled, until suddenly they brought up in front of a high, natural arch of rock, at the top

of which was printed, in large, golden letters:—

THE GLAD LANDS:

Fun and Welcome to All.

The great ostrich set the boy and girl down beneath the arch, and introduced them to the little black bear, who seemed to be waiting for them.

"You must excuse me now," said the ostrich, "I must get ready for the games this after= noon, I will see you later," and he was off among the trees.

"Now for the fun," said the lit= tle black bear,

who parted the hedge in front of them, and led them into a field beyond, where all kinds of animals and birds were playing games, and having a good time, just for all the world like a lot of school boys in vacation.

A big, good=natured lion was teaching a little Guinea=pig to fly a kite.

A troop of kangaroos were playing leap=frog, and a baby hippopotamus was taking a swim in a big pond, while a mis= chievous elephant was squirting water on some polar bears, who seemed to think it great fun to get a ducking.

The lion, when he got the kite up for the Guinea=pig, came and joined Peter, Sue and the little bear, and all four started to see the monkeys, who were playing soldiers, on the parade ground.

It was a funny sight to see the gray whiskered orang=outang, put the young ring=tailed monkeys through their facings.

Dressed as they were, in red coats and white helmets, they certainly looked much like the real soldiers we see on parade.

From the monkeys they went to hear the grand concert by the jungle band which was made up of all the wild animals of the forest. They played the sweetest music ever heard, while the birds furnished a chorus from the trees.

So the four friends made the rounds of that whole

beautiful garden and, wherever they went, they were welcomed and urged to join the play.

Thus they merrily romped away the whole beautiful autumn morning, until the leopard rang the bell for luncheon, when all the jolly animals came trooping to dainty tables spread beneath the trees.

The rhinoceros sat with the gay gazelle; the tiger with the penguin; the crocodile helped the tapir to sugar; and the elephant poured the tea.

After luncheon, a troop of parrots gave a Punch and Judy show, which made way for a pantomime, in which Peter acted the clown and Sue played Columbine, the fairy Princess: the other parts were taken by the ever ready animals.

A porcupine made a few pointed remarks, and a German walrus did a specialty on the French horn. All in all the matinee was a great success.

Later, the animals arranged a vast merry=go=’round under a spreading banyan tree, and Peter and Sue had the best ride of their lives to the music of a great calliope and the combination jungle band.

Peter was mounted on the back of a peli= can. Sue seated herself on a great, good= natured beaver, and away they went.

At first the music was soft and low as they all swung round the banyan tree. But stead= ily the speed increased and finally be= came fast and furious, the music keeping time, but growing faint and far away.

They left the shade of the tree and seemed to be whirling through space, as fainter and slower grew the music.

*　　　*　　　*　　　*　　　*

The red glow of the sunset was behind the apple trees.

A hand=organ played softly below the hill.

And this is the story that was told by Peter Funnybone to his sister Sue and these are the pictures he drew upon his slate.

5 Little Pigs.

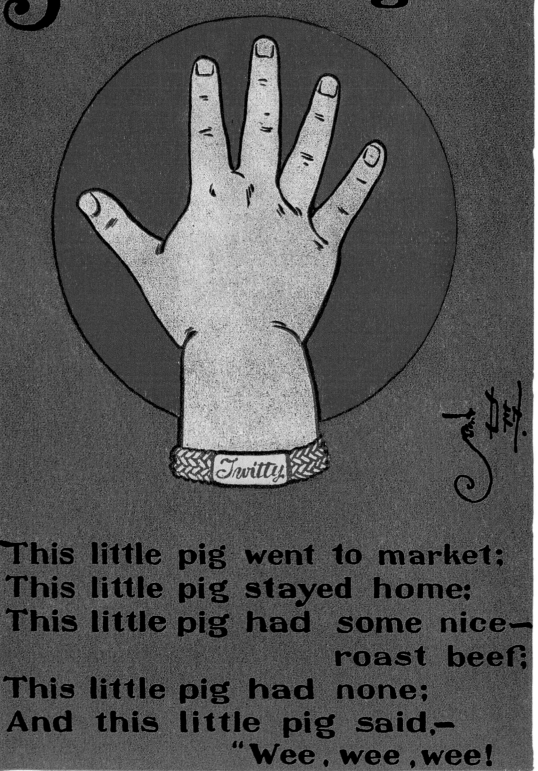

This little pig went to market;
This little pig stayed home:
This little pig had some nice—
         roast beef;
This little pig had none;
And this little pig said,—
         "Wee, wee, wee!
I can't find my way home."

 **T**his
little
pig
went
to
market;

This little pig stayed home;

This
little
pig
had
some
nice
roast beef;

This little pig had none;

And this little pig said.
"Wee, wee, wee !
I can't
find my
way
home."

Inverurie, Paget West,
Bermuda. June Fifth,
1903.